For Tiff and Ben.
—D.D.

immedium
inspiring a world of imagination

Immedium, Inc.
P.O. Box 31846
San Francisco, CA 94131
www.immedium.com

First hardcover edition published 2012.

Edited by Eric Searleman
Book design by Stefanie Liang

Printed in Malaysia
10 9 8 7 6 5 4 3 2 1

ISBN: 978-1-59702-029-9

Library of Congress Cataloging-in-Publication Data

Derrick, David G., 1978-
Animals don't, so I won't / by David Derrick. -- 1st hardcover ed.
p. cm.
Summary: "Benjamin is a young boy who pretends to become different animals to avoid cleaning his room and eating his dinner, so his mother must match his transformations and his wits"--Provided by pub.
ISBN 978-1-59702-029-9 (hardcover)
[1. Behavior--Fiction. 2. Animals--Habits and behavior--Fiction.
3. Mother and child--Fiction. 4. Imagination--Fiction.] I. Title. II. Title: Animals do not, so I will not.
PZ7.D4465An 2012
[E]--dc23

2011052797

By David G. Derrick, Jr.

Immedium, Inc. • San Francisco, CA

Ben loved animals. He had animal toys, games, and books, along with his very own zoo membership. Sometimes he even liked to pretend he was a wild animal.

Benjamin!
It's time to clean up your
toys and get ready for dinner.

Sorry, Mom. I can't because I'm a beetle.
And beetles don't clean up their toys.

You're a beetle?

**Yup.
Beetles
don't,
so I won't.**

Okay. Then
we better start
acting like
beetles...

Beetles are part of nature's clean-up crew.
So if you're a beetle, you'll have to
clean up someone else's mess.

Whose mess?

The elephant's.

YUCK! **Okay, okay, I'll clean up.**

Don't forget to wash your
hands before dinner.

Eat your dinner, Benjamin.

It looks disgusting.

It's lasagna.
Be a good boy
and eat your dinner.

I'm not
a boy...

I'm a penguin, and penguins don't eat lasagna!

If you're a penguin,
then we'll have to
eat like penguins.

Okay,
sounds
good
to me.
Where's
the fish?

BARF!!!
Gross!
All right,
I'll eat
my food!

Ben? Come out.
It's time for your bath.
GRR

No, I won't!

I'm a leopard,
and leopards
don't take baths.

Sure they do.
Leopard mothers use their large,
rough tongues to bathe their little cubs.

What? Ick!
Stop it!
Okay, I'll take a bath.

Remember to wash
behind your ears.

GRUNT! GRUNT!

Sorry, I can't.
I'm a hippo,
and hippos don't use soap.

If you're a hippo, then you'll have to get clean like one.

What are those fish doing?

They're cleaning. Instead of using soap, hippos let barbell fish eat any bugs, bacteria, and dirt off their skin.

Wait, what?
Where are
they going?
All right, I'll
use soap.

It's time to
get dressed dear.

You can't make me
get in my pajamas...

Because I'm a bear,
and bears don't
wear pajamas!

Yes, of course they do, silly. If you're a bear,
then you're already wearing soft, furry pajamas.

Huh?
I am?

Bears have dense coats of fur
to keep them warm and dry.

Okay,
now brush
your teeth, honey.
SNAP!
SNAP!

No, I won't!
I'm a crocodile,
and crocodiles
don't brush their teeth.

Sure they do.
They just use birds
instead of a toothbrush.

Really? Birds in my mouth?
That's too weird! I'll brush my teeth.

Ben, wash your face, please.
No can do, Mom. I'm a shark, and sharks don't wash their faces.

You're right.
Sharks don't wash
their faces, remoras do.

What's a remora?

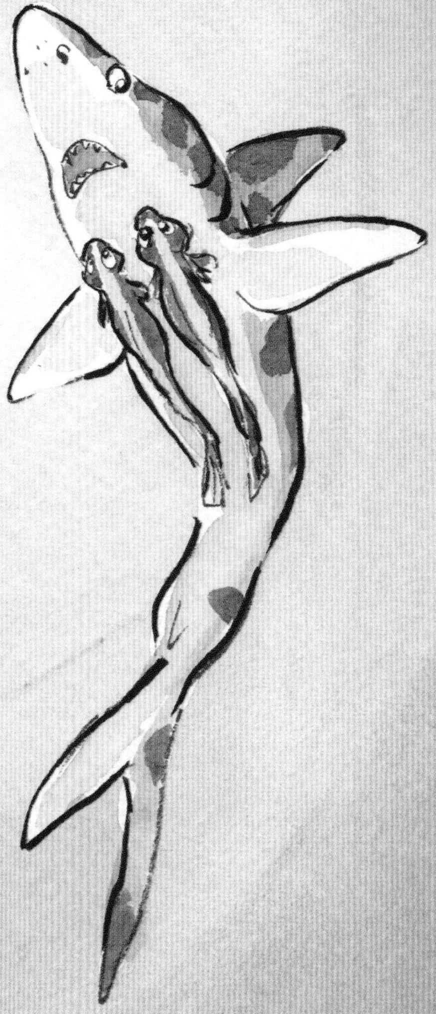

They are fish
that stick to
the bellies
of sharks
and whales.
If there's anything
on your face,
they'll clean it
off for you.

**Fine, then I'm
not a shark.
I'm a...**

Slug!

Come on!
Get up, Benjamin.

I'm so tired,
I can't move.

Good,
it's time for bed.

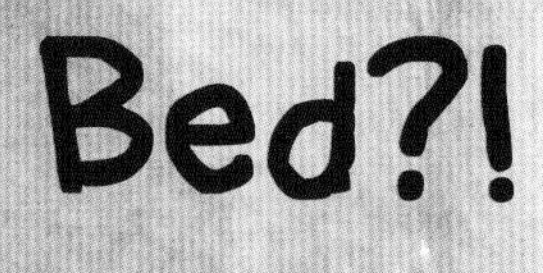

OOHH EEEOOH!
You can't make me go to bed.
I'm a chimp!
Well, mister, I'm not
so sure about that.

Don't you know chimpanzees make
beds every night high in the trees?

They do? But I'm not tired.

Wrapped in a blanket
of leaves, little chimps
are rocked to sleep
by gentle breezes.

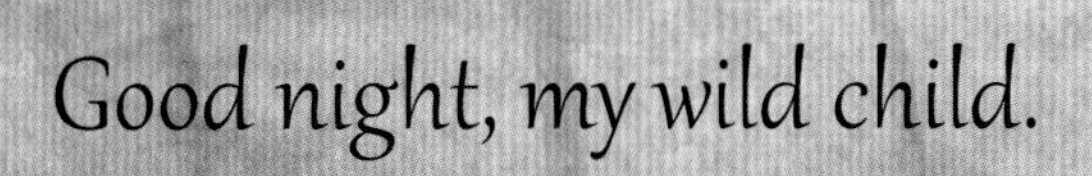

Good night, my wild child.

But early
the next morning...

I'm a rooster,
and roosters don't sleep in.